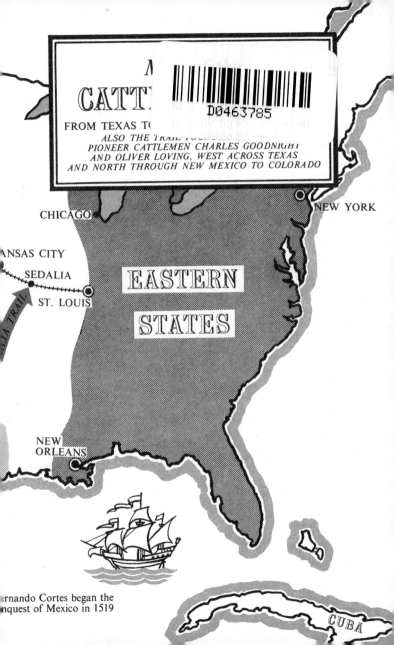

MAP

CATTLE

FROM TEXAS TO

ALSO THE TRAIL FOLLOWED BY
PIONEER CATTLEMEN CHARLES GOODNIGHT
AND OLIVER LOVING, WEST ACROSS TEXAS
AND NORTH THROUGH NEW MEXICO TO COLORADO

D0463785

NEW YORK

CHICAGO

ANSAS CITY

SEDALIA

ST. LOUIS

LIA TRAIL

EASTERN

STATES

NEW
ORLEANS

CUBA

rnando Cortes began the
nquest of Mexico in 1519

INDEX

	Page
The beginning	4
The first Cattle	6
The early Spanish Rancheros	8
The Mexican Vaquero	10
The Mexican Saddle	12
The early Texas Cowboy	14
'For their Hides and Tallow'	16
The Trail Drive	18
Typical Trail Drovers of the 70's and 80's	20
Chaparejos ('Chaps' pronounced 'Shaps')	22
Tapaderos, Spurs and Quirts	24
The Lariat	26
The Texas Longhorn	28
Mustangs and Broncos	30
The Round-up	32
The Chuck Wagon	34
Stampede	36
The end of the Trail	38
The Town Marshal	40
The Colt Six-Shooter	42
The Winchester '73	44
Winter on the Range	46
The Gunfighters	48
The modern Rodeo	50

THE STORY OF THE
COWBOY

written and illustrated
by FRANK HUMPHRIS

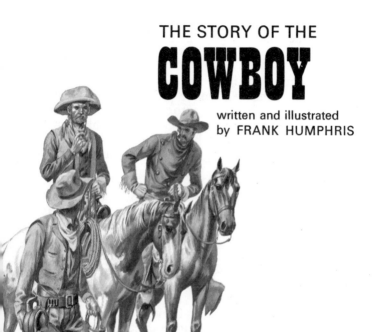

Ladybird Books Loughborough

The beginning

The story of the American cowboy and his equipment began in the year 1519 when Hernando Cortes landed his tiny army on the shores of Mexico, and proceeded to conquer the well-populated land of the Aztec Emperor, Montezuma.

In addition to the 'gentlemen adventurers', men at arms and seamen who made up his 'army' — only 663 persons altogether — he took ashore some sixteen horses for use as cavalry shock troops. This seems an insignificant number, but landing them was an important historical event, for they were the first horses ever to set foot in America.

It is a strange fact of natural history that until the arrival of the Spaniards, there was not a single horse or cow on the American continent.

Never having seen a horse before, the natives thought the armour-clad horsemen were supernatural beings, half human, half animal, and at first were terrified of what seemed to them to be strange new gods. By exploiting such fears, and every other advantage, Cortes and his Conquistadores (Kon-kees-ta-dor-es) overthrew the Aztec Empire, claimed the conquered land for Spain and began the ruthless exploitation of the country's rich mines of gold and silver.

More adventurers arrived. Younger sons of the Spanish nobility sailed from Spain with horses and men, determined to carve their fortunes from the great new lands across the seas.

Astonished Aztecs see the Spanish horsemen for the first time.

4

The first Cattle

Two years after Cortes landed, another historic event occurred. The first horses had already arrived — now came the second essential to the story of the cowboy — cattle!

By then the increasing number of Spaniards on the mainland needed more meat than could be obtained by hunting. They also needed heavy, strong leather for saddles, harness, boots and other equipment, the native buckskin being unsuitable for these purposes.

While most of the adventurers were obsessed with the search for Aztec gold, a certain Gregorio de Villa-lobos saw the possibility of raising cattle in New Spain, as Mexico was then called. The climate of the foothills and uplands of the new country was not unlike that of the cattle-rearing provinces of western Spain, and there seemed no reason why a virile and adaptable breed of cattle should not prosper.

The first shipment that Villalobos took to the main-land was a little group of calves. No one knows for certain just how many; one account mentions seven — six heifers and a young bull — but their destiny was great, for they were the first of the strain that eventually produced the great cattle herds of the American West.

Villalobos lands the first cattle on the American continent.

The early Spanish Rancheros

The small, wiry Spanish cattle thrived on the lush grass of the Mexican plains, and their numbers rapidly increased. It was not long before other Spaniards saw the advantage of having cattle grazing over large areas of land which could later be claimed for themselves. More cattle were imported and more ranches established.

Herdsmen were required for the growing number of herds, and so, some time during the first half of the sixteenth century, the first American cowhands appeared.

Of course, they looked very different from the cowboys of the western States that we are accustomed to seeing in films.

At first the cattle were in fenced pastures and handled by herdsmen carrying pikes, or 'picas', in the same way as the bulls are handled in Spain even today. These picas were later discarded as the cattle spread to the open ranges and the lariat was used instead.

To protect him from the brush, and the thorns of the cactus, the cowhand attached to his saddle a sort of apron made of big flaps of leather. These were called 'armas', meaning armour, and could be folded back over the rider's legs.

The unusual stirrups were carved from a solid piece of hardwood with only a small hole for the toes.

8   *Early Spanish rancheros with their picas and armas.*

The Mexican Vaquero

During the next 250 years the technique of 'ranching' — that is, raising cattle on open, unfenced ranges, with seasonal round-ups and branding — was developed on the ranches that were established in Mexico and as far north as what are now California and Nevada in the present United States.

The cowboy, or vaquero as he was called (from the Spanish word 'vaca' — meaning cow), now began to look more like our idea of the typical Mexican cowhand.

On his head was a huge, wide-brimmed sombrero; a short jacket, sometimes decorated with braid, was worn over a cotton shirt. The 'armas' were no longer used, his legs being protected with tight leather leggings known as 'chaparejos' fastened down the sides with buttons and loops. The old, round, wooden 'toe' stirrups of the earlier saddles became large and box-shaped.

A colourful serape, or poncho, a dual purpose blanket, was tied behind the saddle. From the high pommel of the saddle hung a coiled lariat, the tool of the cowboy's trade.

The Mexican vaquero had become the complete cowboy. Over the years his equipment, clothing, saddle, bridle, boots, spurs and lariat had altered and developed until they were completely functional, each perfect for its purpose.

A typical Mexican Vaquero.

The Mexican Saddle

The most important single item of equipment for the Mexican cowhand was his saddle.

The stresses and strains of roping cattle demanded a saddle of special design and great strength, and to enable a man to live and work in it from dawn to dusk it had to be large and comfortable. Over the decades the Mexicans had developed a saddle to meet their requirements.

Its most prominent features were the large horn mounted on the raised pommel (front) of the saddle — the large leather 'cantinas', or saddle bags, and the very wide, strong 'cincha', the Mexican name for girth. This was the basic, functional design from which all later cowboy saddles developed.

The underlying shape was made of wood covered with heavy, wet rawhide, which shrank as it dried and made a framework of great strength. Rawhide would have been most uncomfortable to ride on, so over this went the ordinary leather fittings, either plain or embossed like the superb Mexican show saddle shown in the illustration.

The early American pioneers found this type of saddle ideal and obtained them from the Santa Fe traders, Americans who had opened-up an overland trade route to the town of Santa Fe in New Mexico. In the course of time the Texas cowboy, always an individualist, made alterations to fit his own ideas of riding and roping.

Silver-mounted saddle horn

Pommel

Cantinas *(Saddle Bags)*

Cincha *(Girth)*

Stirrup Leathers

A FINE SILVER MOUNTED MEXICAN SHOW SADDLE

TEXAS COWBOY SADDLE

The large 'cantinas' have disappeared, the horn is smaller and the seat improved. A flank cinch is added, while the narrow pommel is now built with a 'swell' to provide a grip for the rider's legs.

Cantle

Swell Forks *(Pommel)*

Horn

Skirts

Saddle Strings

Flank Cinch

Cinch *(Girth)*

Wooden Stirrup

The early Texas Cowboy

Until 1836 Texas was a part of Mexico. In that year the Anglo-American settlers who had moved into Texas, rose in revolt against the corrupt Mexican government and, after defeating the Mexican army, declared Texas a republic.

In the troubled times that followed, many Mexican cattlemen abandoned their Texas ranches and returned to Mexico. They left behind thousands of cattle roaming their former ranges. The ranges were then, of course, taken over by the Anglo-Americans.

As the Americans — or Texans, as we should now call them — took over, they adopted both the methods and the equipment of the vaqueros. And so the first Texas cowboys came into being.

It was a wild, primitive country in those days. There were only a few small towns such as San Antonio and Austin. Most were merely settlements with outlying farms and ranches, and these only in certain areas. Beyond them was the vast emptiness of the great plains — the hunting ground of the dreaded Comanche Indians.

The Texans, dressed in simple, homespun clothing or buckskin, for cloth was scarce, set about raising their cattle and hogs. They rode with a rifle near to hand, a pistol and Bowie knife at their belts, and kept a watchful eye open for raiding Indian war parties or vengeful Mexicans.

An early Texas cowhand in buckskins, with muzzle-loading rifle and Bowie knife.

'For their Hides and Tallow'

During the years that followed, the long-horned cattle thrived in the river valleys of southern Texas, and in the course of time the Texan ranch owner found himself with more cattle than he knew what to do with. His problem was the lack of markets to which he could sell them.

Over a thousand miles of wilderness separated Texas from the large cities of the north. The teeming gold-mining camps of California were equally remote, with vast deserts and mountain ranges in between.

Only a few brave ranchers attempted such a long cattle drive. One who did so took two years to reach California. Others lost their herds and left their bones on unknown trails.

A growing demand for hides and tallow for the leather and candle industries provided one market, however. At that time the paraffin oil lamp was an expensive luxury, and in most homes candles or simple tallow lamps were the usual form of lighting.

Small 'factories' for rendering down the tallow sprang up in the coastal areas, and large numbers of hides, hoofs and horns found buyers among the leather and glue manufacturers. But it was a melancholy sight indeed for the cattleman, for no-one wanted the meat itself and thousands of skinned carcases were simply left for the wolves and buzzards.

Then in 1861 came the terrible war between the States.

Some of the first ranch-houses and cabins to be built out on the great plains were simply made from clods of earth, for timber was very scarce. Thick, heavy turves were placed brickwise to form the walls. Poles covered with brushwood with turf laid on top formed the roof.

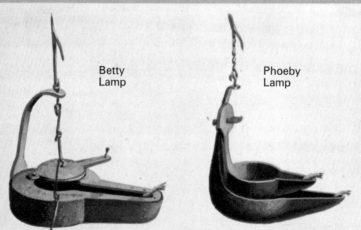

Betty Lamp

Phoeby Lamp

TALLOW OR GREASE BURNING LAMPS

Before paraffin was available, either candles or grease (tallow) burning lamps were used in the early ranch-houses.

The Trail Drive

It was after the Civil War ended, in 1866, that the great cattle drives to the north began. The defeat of the South left Texas virtually bankrupt, its only wealth being the countless thousands of cattle running wild over the ranges. In fact at that time the cattle outnumbered the human population by six to one!

However, the booming industrial cities of the north and east were demanding more and more beef. The first cattle drives which attempted to meet this demand were not successful. The main difficulties were only overcome when an enterprising meat buyer, J. G. McCoy, arranged for the newly built railroad to run a branch line from Kansas City to Abilene specially for transporting cattle. This shortened the drive by hundreds of miles.

The trail that led to Abilene became famous as the Chisholm Trail. The long drive — it was still some 900 miles — crossed Indian territory, wound through rocky 'dry' areas, over broken scrub-land and scorching plains. The rivers that had to be crossed were sometimes in flood, adding further dangers to the long drive.

It was a testing time for even the toughest cowboy. Each day he was up before dawn and in the saddle, slowly easing the herd along through the hours of daylight. At night he had to take his turn riding as night guard!

A trail drive.

Typical Trail Drovers of the 70's and 80's

The 1870's and 1880's were the hey-day of the American cowboy! During the season, commencing each spring, the herds poured north from Texas to such cow-towns as Abilene, Ellsworth, Wichita and Dodge City.

Some idea of the numbers involved may be gathered from the figures for 1876 when 322,000 cattle were driven to Dodge and Ellis.

The typical herd numbered between 2,000 and 3,500 steers, rarely more because of the difficulty of handling too large a number. Such a herd needed from eight to twelve drovers, plus the trail 'boss' and the cook. Each man had a string of six or eight horses, so a horse 'wrangler' had to be included — the man who looked after all the horses.

Most of the stories and films about the West deal with this period, so let us see what the cowboy of that time really looked like. The majority wore moustaches, for these were fashionable, and quite a few also had beards.

Two items which every cowboy wore, but which have now largely disappeared, were the big neck scarf, or bandana, and gauntlet gloves frequently fringed at the sides. Shirts were usually of heavy flannel in some serviceable colour. You will notice that the furthest cowboy in the illustration is wearing a shirt with a shield front, a popular style at the time.

Typical trail drovers of the 70's and 80's.

Chaparejos ('Chaps'—pronounced 'Shaps')

One of the most striking items of cowboy gear are the heavy leather leggings commonly known as 'chaps'.

Chaparejos, to give them their full Mexican name, are in three main styles, the earliest being the closed-leg type. These are usually known as 'shot-gun' chaps, as the two closed legs resemble the twin barrels of a shot-gun. Quite often they have decorative fringes down the sides.

Naturally these were awkward to get on and off, and the wrap-around 'batwing' style soon took over in popularity. With these, each side consisted of a large piece of leather which folded round the rider's leg and clipped together leaving a flap, or wing, at the side. The clips are where you see the line of conchos or rosettes. Batwing chaps were easy to remove. The cowboy just unclipped each leg, unbuckled the waist belt and off they came!

On the northern ranges, where winter temperatures can drop below zero, woolly chaps were very popular. They were usually made from Angora goatskin, but sheep, wolf and bearskin were other possible sources.

The illustration shows how each separate leg was attached to a half belt which buckled round the back of the waist. A leather thong or lacing joined the chaps together at the front.

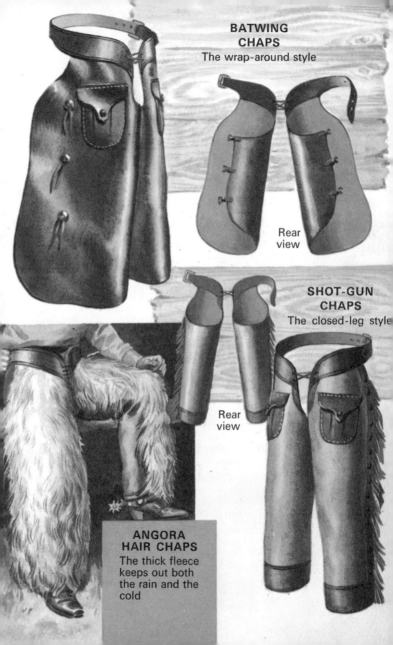

BATWING CHAPS
The wrap-around style

Rear view

SHOT-GUN CHAPS
The closed-leg style

Rear view

ANGORA HAIR CHAPS
The thick fleece keeps out both the rain and the cold

Tapaderos, Spurs and Quirts

Tapaderos, or 'Taps' for short, are leather hoods that fit over the stirrups. They were a typical part of the early Texas cowboy saddles and, indeed, the U.S. Army saddles were also fitted with them. However, the army ones were plain and simple; the cowboys' were in many shapes and sizes.

There were 'Eagle Bill' taps, so called because the front was shaped like the face of an eagle with long, down-sweeping sidepieces elaborately carved and decorated when used for show purposes. Other simpler styles included some that were closed-in underneath and lined with sheepskin for use in cold climates.

The large spurs worn by the cowboys look more ferocious than they are, for the points of the rowels are quite blunt. Like the other equipment they are based on the traditional Mexican spurs, but are strapped on the boot just below the ankle. The vaquero wore his on the boot heel itself. The shank, which was usually about $2\frac{1}{2}$ inches long, had a downward curve and a small projection to keep the chaps from catching in the rowel.

In the old days no cowboy was complete without a quirt dangling from his waist by a loop. This was a short pliable whip of plaited rawhide. Strangely enough, they have now gone out of fashion together with the fringed gauntlet gloves that were formerly popular.

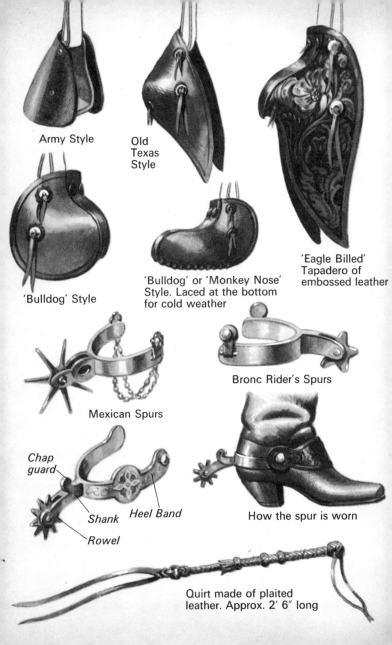

Army Style

Old Texas Style

'Bulldog' Style

'Bulldog' or 'Monkey Nose' Style. Laced at the bottom for cold weather

'Eagle Billed' Tapadero of embossed leather

Mexican Spurs

Bronc Rider's Spurs

Chap guard

Shank

Rowel

Heel Band

How the spur is worn

Quirt made of plaited leather. Approx. 2' 6" long

The Lariat

Most of the lariats used today are made from manila, one of the vegetable fibres similar to hemp or sisal. The original lariat used by the early Mexican vaqueros was a long rope made from plaited rawhide.

The origins of roping are obscure; no-one knows precisely when it developed but, some time during the three centuries since Villalobos introduced the first cattle, the vaquero became an expert at handling the flying loop. It was a most useful tool and provided the only really practical way of catching semi-wild cattle on the open ranges.

The word 'lariat' is a corruption of the Spanish 'la reata', meaning 'the rope'. The name 'lasso', so often used by easterners but never by the cowboys, is just the noose at the end of the rope.

There are two methods of roping, the 'hard and fast' and the 'dally' style. In the former the rope is fastened to the saddle, while in the latter the roper takes the strain by making a few quick turns, or 'dallies', round the saddle horn to 'snub' the rope after making his catch. Leather reatas are always used in this way.

The experts practised many wonderful throws, making the loop catch the steer's forefeet, or the hind-feet only, or even forming a figure '8' to snare both at the same time.

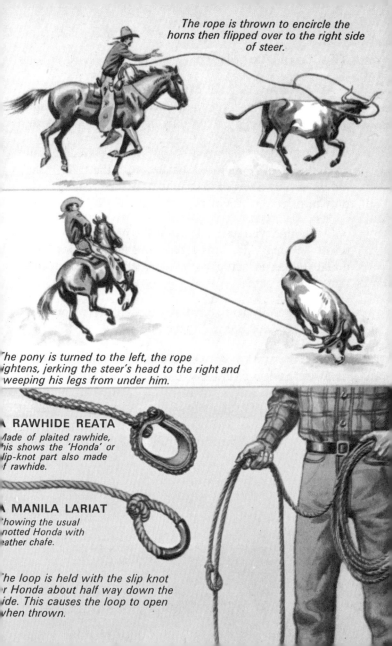

The rope is thrown to encircle the horns then flipped over to the right side of steer.

The pony is turned to the left, the rope tightens, jerking the steer's head to the right and sweeping his legs from under him.

A RAWHIDE REATA
Made of plaited rawhide, this shows the 'Honda' or slip-knot part also made of rawhide.

A MANILA LARIAT
Showing the usual knotted Honda with leather chafe.

The loop is held with the slip knot or Honda about half way down the side. This causes the loop to open when thrown.

The Texas Longhorn

As we have read, the cattle originally brought over from Spain thrived on the American grasslands, and over the centuries grew not only in numbers but in size.

Unfortunately, the breed is now almost extinct. Of all the millions of Longhorns that went up the trail in the old days, only a few of their kind now survive and those only in private parks or zoos.

Living like wild animals out in the brush, they themselves became wild, long-legged and fleet of foot and, unlike domestic cattle, were more ready to turn and fight than to run.

They certainly had something to fight with, for they grew tremendous horns — hence the name, 'Longhorn'.

While the average horn spread was probably 4–5 feet, many were 6 feet or more, one record specimen reaching the astonishing length of nearly 8 feet. The average Longhorn weighed around 900 lbs when about five years old. An older steer could reach as much as 1,500 lbs. but far too much of him was bone, gristle and tough, stringy meat.

Once the ranches were established and the cattle trade developed, these bad-tempered, tough and ugly cattle were replaced by other breeds such as Herefords and Shorthorns. These produce more and better quality beef than the Longhorn.

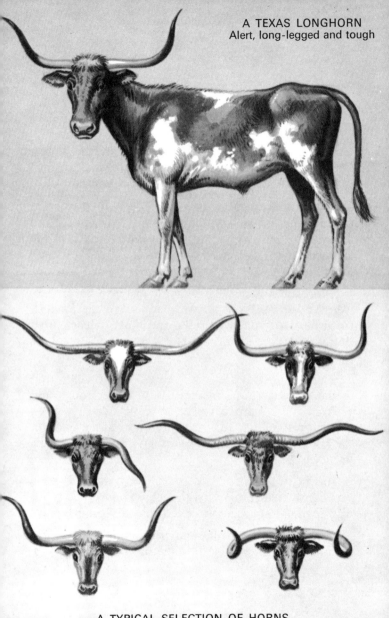

A TEXAS LONGHORN
Alert, long-legged and tough

A TYPICAL SELECTION OF HORNS

Mustangs and Broncos

Great herds of wild mustangs once roamed the western plains. They were descendants of the horses originally introduced by the Spaniards. Small, from 12 to 14 hands in height, rough, scraggy and of uncertain temper, they were remarkably courageous and tough. Once broken in and trained they were ideal for ranch work, and in fact were the original 'cow ponies'.

Wild horse hunters, or mustangers as they were called, hunted these herds of mustangs. Having captured a number they would either sell them unbroken to the ranches, or themselves break them in as saddle horses, thereby obtaining a better price.

Unbroken horses, whether mustangs or other breeds, were known as broncos or broncs, from the Spanish word meaning rough or rude, and most ranches hired professional bronco-busters for the job of 'breaking them in'.

There were, and are, many ways of doing this, and in the old days some methods were rather rough and ready, the usual procedure being to slap a heavy stock saddle on the horse's back, climb on and stay on until the horse was exhausted and gave up the effort to throw its rider.

This treatment was repeated each day until the horse was considered 'broken', although obviously the result was anything but a gentle or well-mannered horse!

Nowadays far more time and care is taken, particularly with horses born and bred on the ranch.

The bronco-buster at work.

The Round-up

The big round-ups took place in spring and autumn. The spring round-up was the more important for it was then that the spring calves received their owner's brand. The autumn round-up was necessary to gather the beef herd for late markets and, of course, brand any calves born since the previous round-up.

Usually the ranches co-operated, each providing a 'team'. By helping one another the work could be done more efficiently and cattle that had strayed from one ranch to another could be claimed. The crews worked different sections of the range in turn.

As the hills and valleys, wooded areas, canyons and brush were combed, small groups of cattle grew into bigger groups all heading towards the round-up ground.

Next day the 'cutting out', or separating of the bulls and steers from the cows and calves began. Anything that carried a brand was kept in the one herd, while the other unbranded stock was attended to.

Branding was necessary to establish the ownership in a land where originally no fences existed. A cowboy on his best 'cutting' pony would work a calf to the outside of the herd where it was roped and quickly dragged over towards the fire. Here the 'flankers' grabbed the struggling, kicking animal, threw it on its side and held it while the owner's brand was applied and any necessary doctoring and innoculation took place.

Rounding-up and branding calves.

The Chuck Wagon

Any working men constantly on the move require feeding, and cowboys are no exception.

Charles Goodnight, a famous rancher and trail driver, is said to have invented the chuck wagon, a sort of mobile canteen which followed the cowboys on the various round-ups and, of course, accompanied the herds on the long trail drives to the north.

It was a fairly large, sturdy wagon with a sort of crude kitchen dresser built at the back with the shelves and cupboards facing rearwards.

The door of this cupboard — which was also the tail gate of the wagon — let down horizontally and formed a working table for the cook.

The staple diet was pork (bacon), beans and sour-dough biscuits, and to drink there was coffee, black and strong and so thick that the spoon stood upright — at least that is how the old hands said they liked it! A supply of flour and salt and possibly sugar or molasses (black treacle) was also carried. There was beef ready to hand, of course, if fresh meat was required.

Inside the wagon were the cook's pots and pans and a Dutch oven, the mens' tin cups and plates, bed-rolls, spare clothing, branding-irons, ropes, tarpaulins and, in fact, all the gear necessary for the trail and camp.

A typical chuck wagon.

Stampede

One of the worst dangers of the trail drives was a stampede, particularly one that took place at night.

Summer storms with thunder and lightning were dreaded, as the cattle, already restless and nervy, were more than usually ready to bolt in blind, desperate panic at a sudden vivid flash of lightning or violent crash of thunder overhead.

So wild were the Longhorns that almost anything would set them off. An unexpected noise, the sharp crack of a dead branch stepped on by a pony, even a loose tumbleweed blowing along in the night breeze could send a startled animal leaping to its feet with a bound and a snort, perhaps setting the whole herd off in a mindless, headlong rush.

On nights such as these, the crew slept fully dressed with their horses ready saddled nearby, for woe betide any cowboy who got in the way of those thousands of pounding hooves.

It was useless to try to stop the fear-crazed beasts. All the men could do was to gallop at top speed until the herd strung out, and then try to force the leading steers to swing into a wide curve until eventually the whole herd was running in a circle. After a while, exhaustion would bring them to a halt.

Cowboys attempting to swing the leading steers into a wide curve.

36

The End of the Trail

After nearly a thousand miles in the saddle — and three months of heat and dust and bawling cattle, the end of the trail was reached.

The cattle were sold and loaded onto the train, the cowhands were paid off, and with ear-splitting war-whoops they raced off to town.

Those early cow-towns were crude, ramshackle collections of buildings, mostly one storey but often with two-storey false fronts. A large number of saloons with dance halls and gambling tables catered for the entertainment of the trail crews. General stores, boarding houses and a hotel or two for the cattle buyers and ranchers made up the rest of the 'town'.

On arriving the cowboys took the first layer of dust from their throats at the nearest saloon, then visited the barber's for a haircut and a general clean-up after the weeks of living in the open.

Next came sorely needed shopping to replace worn and ragged clothing. Then, with three months' wages in their pockets, the cowboys looked around for some relaxation. There was little choice.

The saloons offered company, drinks, cards and other games of chance where the stakes were high. Or the dance halls could be visited for a 'hoe dig with the calico queens', an expressive phrase which described their bow-legged gyrations round the floor more accurately than the word 'dancing'.

For a few hectic days and nights the cowboys forgot the hardships and loneliness of the trail — then it was time to return down the long miles home!

*An evening's relaxation before the long trail
back to the range.*

The Town Marshal

By any standards, the job of a frontier marshal or sheriff was tough, dangerous and often fatally short-lived. Many of the frontier towns were hundreds of miles from any established system of law and order, and once enough people settled in an area, or a 'town' grew large enough, it was up to the local population to organise their own law. This meant finding someone not only able but willing to undertake the task.

With no organised police force to help him, the sheriff was expected to uphold the law and maintain reasonable order, however informal, in a community which might include rustlers, thieves and outlaws, all of whom carried guns and considered him more or less fair game.

It was inevitable, therefore, that many marshals were chosen because of their own ability to use a six-gun effectively, their deadly reputation helping to discourage the more enthusiastic trouble makers.

Some of the most noted (and notorious) gunmen in the West, wore the silver star at one time or another; 'Wild Bill' Hickok, Bat Masterson, Bill Tilghman, 'Mysterious Dave' Mather, Wyatt Earp, John Slaughter, Pat Garrett and even Ben Thomson — to name but a few.

Some were little or no better than the toughs themselves; others brought law and order to the West with courage and honesty — and many met their deaths in doing so.

Most films, for some reason, picture the sheriff or marshal dressed in the everyday working clothes of a cowhand straight off the ranch, but in the larger communities it was a responsible and comparatively well-paid position, and most law men dressed in ordinary town clothes. Frock coats were popular at this time and, of course, riding boots were worn as the horse was the main form of transport.

A typical trail town marshal.

The Colt Six-Shooter

Having referred to the Town Marshal, we can now consider the guns used in the West.

Sam Colt began the manufacture of his famous revolvers in 1836. The Texas Rangers found the new weapon ideal for frontier fighting, and Colt followed with a series of models that were notable for their power and balance. The earliest were percussion, or 'cap and ball' pistols, for those were the days before metallic cartridges. Each chamber in the cylinder was loaded from the front, or muzzle end, with powder and a bullet, the latter being rammed home with the lever hinged under the barrel. Small copper caps containing fulminate of mercury were then placed on the nipples at the rear of each cylinder. These caps formed the primer, exploding when struck by the hammer and firing the main charges in the chambers.

Though slow to load, they were formidable and accurate weapons and continued in use until the cartridge-firing 'Peacemaker' was introduced in 1873.

Incidentally, this slow reloading was the main reason for many frontiersmen carrying two revolvers — not to shoot both at once!

The most famous Colt revolver was the .45 calibre Colt Single Action Army model of 1873, and this is the gun you see used in practically every Western film. Generally known as the 'Peacemaker', 'Frontier' (in .44 cal.), 'Thumb-buster', 'Hogleg' etc., it was made in all calibres, the most popular in the West being the .45 and .44.

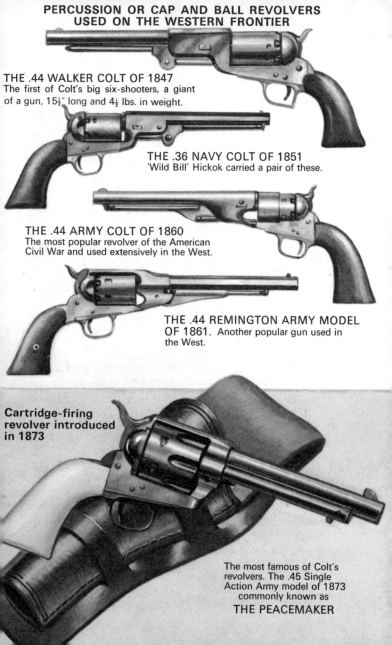

PERCUSSION OR CAP AND BALL REVOLVERS
USED ON THE WESTERN FRONTIER

THE .44 WALKER COLT OF 1847
The first of Colt's big six-shooters, a giant
of a gun, 15½″ long and 4½ lbs. in weight.

THE .36 NAVY COLT OF 1851
'Wild Bill' Hickok carried a pair of these.

THE .44 ARMY COLT OF 1860
The most popular revolver of the American
Civil War and used extensively in the West.

**THE .44 REMINGTON ARMY MODEL
OF 1861.** Another popular gun used in
the West.

**Cartridge-firing
revolver introduced
in 1873**

The most famous of Colt's
revolvers. The .45 Single
Action Army model of 1873
commonly known as

THE PEACEMAKER

The Winchester '73

The forerunner of the Winchester was the Henry rifle, developed during the Civil War. It was a fifteen-shot repeater carrying the cartridges in a tube under the barrel. To men used to the slow clumsiness of a muzzle loader it seemed like a gift from the gods. "You could load it on a Sunday and fire all the week" as one enthusiast said.

In 1866 the Henry firm's name was changed to 'Winchester Repeating Arms Company', and the first rifle bearing Winchester's name appeared that year. Although a considerable improvement over the Henry, it still suffered from the same drawback — it fired rimfire cartridges! Owing to the construction of the brass for these, the powder charge had to be kept low, otherwise the case expanded and jammed the mechanism. It was not until the centre-fire cartridge was perfected that this problem was overcome.

The new model designed to take the centre-fire cartridge was the famous Winchester '73. It was the first, highly accurate, lever action repeater and put Winchester firmly in the lead in rifle manufacture.

Holding fifteen 44-40 calibre cartridges it quickly became a favourite in the West, for it was ideal for frontier conditions, particularly in the 20″ barrel carbine version which made a perfect saddle gun.

Known as "the gun that won the West", it was used by scouts, hunters, cowboys and plainsmen of every description and was so popular that the Colt company chambered their equally famous Frontier Model six-shooter to take the same ammunition.

THE WINCHESTER RIFLE
Model of 1873

The most popular rifle on the frontier. Below, two ranch hands open fire on a group of rustlers caught altering the brands.

Winter on the Range

The climate in the United States varies greatly, from the heat of the semi-arid and desert areas of the south west, to the below zero winter temperatures of the northern plains. Periods of drought also added to the cattlemen's problems.

There was a great cattle boom following the Civil War but during these years there were numerous droughts and freeze-ups. The greatest disaster of all occurred in 1886. After an autumn of unusually fine warm weather, the first snow fell late in the year, then in January the greatest blizzard in living memory struck the northwest.

A hurricane wind drove a choking smother of frozen snow over the cattle ranges. The cattle drifted helplessly with it, for it was almost impossible to breathe without turning away from the wind. Many wandered up to fences where they were later found frozen to death in heaps.

In the canyons and coulees, drifts up to a hundred feet hid the carcases of thousands of others, while more were found trapped in the ice of snow-blanketed rivers. Just how many cowboys died trying to help the cattle no one knows. Many small ranchers and settlers — whole families in some cases — were found frozen to death in their cabins.

Hundreds of ranchers were ruined. The O.S. Bar lost nearly all its stock of 11,000 cattle; in western Kansas 500 survived out of a herd of 5,500.

The wild, free days of the open range were gone. The disaster brought in a more sober, businesslike approach to stock-raising.

The grim, hard life of a cowboy in winter.

The Gunfighters

The Western films we see on T.V. and the cinema are mainly responsible for most people's ideas of the Western frontier. Almost every film features the gunfighter — the man lightning-fast on the draw — and one wonders how much of this general expertise really existed. It would seem that the true state of affairs was very different.

In the first place, although most men went armed for their own protection, not all were expert. Few would have had the time, or been able to afford the ammunition, to enable them to put in the hours of regular practice necessary to develop the split-second speed and accuracy of the film heroes. However this applies to the majority. There were some notable exceptions.

Just as some men are able to run or swim faster than others, become great tennis players or wizards with a football, so some have outstanding natural ability with a gun. 'Wild Bill' Hickok, Wes Hardin and the Sundance Kid were among these exceptional men. Others, such as Jesse James and Billy the Kid, gained their reputations more by their willingness to kill.

There were occasions when quarrels over water rights, or between cattle and sheep-men, exploded into range wars, but most gun fights were sordid affairs — sudden quarrels perhaps over a game of cards.

Card-sharpers infested the saloons, and an accusation of cheating meant reaching for a gun at the same time — after which there was usually another permanent resident for 'Boot Hill' (the local burial ground) in the morning.

A tragic end to a game of cards.

The modern Rodeo

The 'Wild West' of the old days has long since passed into history; the rip-roaring cow-towns are now quiet and peaceful, the cattle trails ploughed under.

However, huge ranches still raise cattle for the nation's markets. Whereas in the old days a cowboy needed little more than a horse and a rope as equipment, beef production is now scientifically studied with the help of computers!

None the less, cowboys still work on the ranches, and, in spite of modern methods, still dress very similarly and perform many of the tasks as in the past.

For those with special skills the great rodeos offer golden opportunities. From the simple contests arranged by cowboys to decide which of the neighbouring ranches had the best riders and ropers, the rodeo has grown into big business. Top performers in the championship class can earn large sums travelling the rodeo circuits.

The contests include bronc riding, steer riding, trick roping and steer roping, a chuck wagon race and the spectacular 'bulldogging' illustrated opposite. In this, the cowboy races alongside the steer, launches himself from the saddle onto the steer's horns, and throws the animal by twisting its head down. The competitor wins who achieves this in the shortest time.

Rodeos will always be popular as long as people have an interest in the cowboy and seek to retain the adventurous spirit of the Old West.

'Bulldogging' a steer.

A Dictionary of Cowboy Terms

ADOBE (Spanish) Dried mud bricks. A building made from these.

ARROYO (Spanish) Dry creek or gully.

BANDANA (Spanish) A large neckerchief usually made of coloured cotton.

BRONCO (Spanish) An unbroken, rough or wild horse.

BUCKAROO A cowboy. A corruption of the Spanish word 'vaquero'. In Spanish the letter 'v' is often pronounced as a soft 'b'; hence vaquero becomes, bakero—buckero—buckeroo.

BURRO (Spanish) A pack donkey.

BUTTES (French) Rocky hills with steep, precipitous sides.

CALABOOSE (Spanish–calabozo) The jail.

CAVVYARD or CAVVY Northern cowboy's term for the horse herd.

CAYUSE A horse. Named after the Cayuse tribe of Indians.

CHAPARRAL (Spanish) A dense thicket of small trees, cactus, brush and entangling vines and creepers.

CHAPS (Spanish–chaparejos, sometimes spelt chaparreras) Leather leggings worn to protect legs from the chaparral.

CINCHA (Spanish) The saddle girth.

CONCHOS (Spanish) Metal or leather discs used for fastening and decoration.